W9-BDC-907

This book is dedicated to
Mikey, Marc, Ryan, Chris, and Seth
who went into the fray
and fought the dragons...

Mikey and the Dragons is published under Jocko Publishing, a sectionalized division in association with Di Angelo Publications INC.

JOCKO PUBLISHING
In association with Di Angelo Publications
4265 San Felipe #1100
Houston, Texas, 77027

Mikey and the Dragons Copyright 2018 Jocko Willink. Illustrated by Jon Bozak.
In digital and print distribution in the United States of America.

Manufactured in North America

www.jockopublishing.com

www.diangelopublications.com

Library of congress cataloging-in-publications data
Mikey and the Dragons. Downloadable via Kindle, iBooks and NOOK.

Library of Congress Registration

Hardback

ISBN-10: 1-942549-43-1

ISBN-13: 978-1-942549-43-7

Facilitated by: Di Angelo Publications

Designed and illustrated by: Jon Bozak

First Edition

10 9 8 7 6 4 5 3 2

No part of this book may be copied or distributed without the author and publisher's written and approved permission. For educational and entertainment purposes, this book may be ordered in bulk through Di Angelo Publications.

1. Children's fiction

2. Children's Fiction ——Narrative ——United States of America with int. Distribution.

MIKEY
AND THE
DRAGONS

BY JOCKO WILLINK
DRAWINGS BY JON BOZAK

JOCKO PUBLISHING

There once was a little boy named Mike,
And there were many things in the world that he didn't like.

He was scared of spiders and beetles and bugs,
And always thought they hid under the rugs.

They were creepy and crawly and nasty and mean,
And he ran from every bug he had ever seen.

But it wasn't only insects that gave Mikey a scare.
There were many other things for which Mike didn't care.

He left the light on when he went to sleep at night.
He was scared there were monsters ready to bite.

Hidden in his closet or under his bed,
He thought they might get him when he lay down his head.

He imagined a monster with giant teeth and claws,
grabbing his neck with its giant paws.

And if it wasn't monsters coming to take him away,
It would be slimy snakes slithering his way.

Yes, Mikey was scared of evil snakes too,
He was horrified of what they could do.

They could sneak in the house and hide in his drawer,
And then bite him to bits, of that he was sure!

There were many other things that gave Mikey a scare,
Which meant there were many things that he wouldn't dare.

He didn't like the water or to go for a swim,
He was scared that giant sharks might come and get him.

He didn't like the playground, with ladders and slides.
He thought if he fell off he would surely die.

Yes, as you can see, things for Mikey were bad,
And being afraid made Mike very sad.

Because so many things scared Mike to the bone,
It turns out that Mikey was often alone.

He would sit by himself and look at the sky,
And then he would quietly ask himself, **Why?**

Why did so many things give him a scare?
How could he ever overcome all that fear?

How could he ever stand up and be brave?
Or would being afraid always make him a slave?

And then one day, Mikey noticed a book.
He opened it up and took a quick look.

It had pictures of dragons with fangs like a snake,
And all kinds of scary things that made Mikey shake.

But in the pictures, there was a boy too,
Who didn't look scared, but like he knew what to do.

And even though Mikey was scared indeed,
He decided that he would give the book a read.

He opened the first page, which he eagerly read,
And this is what the dragon book said...

THE
DRAGON
PRINCE

THE DRAGON PRINCE

AS TOLD BY

SIR JAKE

KNIGHT OF THE SEA AIR AND LAND

There once was a kingdom long ago and far away.
And the kingdom had suffered a horrible day.

Their protector and leader, their King, he had died.
And when they found out, the whole village cried.

When the King was alive, he was a powerful force,
Now they took the dead King away by carriage and horse.

They knew they would miss him and that made them sad,
But there was something else that made them feel bad.

The King had always been so strong and brave,
And protected the kingdom from the Dragon Cave.

The Dragon Cave was just over the hill,
And filled with scary creatures that were ready to kill!

Horrible dragons of every single type,
Who thought people in the kingdom were especially ripe.

The people thought the dragons had breath of fire,
And that the dragons stood twenty feet tall or higher.

They thought the dragons had sword-stopping scales,
And powerful, long, razor-sharp tails.

But the brave King never let the beasts around,
He stood up and fought and held his ground.

And as long as the King had been the King,
None of the dragons could do a thing.

Yes, the King always kept the dragons at bay,
By going out bravely into the fray.

It seemed without fear the King would go fight,
He'd beat the dragons and come home at night.

But now that the King had died and was gone,
There was only one person to fight and carry on.

But that person wasn't big or mighty or strong,
In fact, he hadn't been alive that long.

Now the person who had dragons to chase,
Was just a little boy with a smiling face.

Yes, the person that must now stand up and be bold,
Was just the little Prince who was only seven years old.

And the people in the village just couldn't be sure,
That this young boy, the little Prince, could endure.

How could someone so young and so small,
Stand up to the mighty dragons that were so tall?

And the Prince himself, he also didn't know,
If he had the courage it would take to go.

Because he was so little and small and young,
He didn't know if he could get the job done.

How could he make the mean dragons yield,
When he could barely lift a sword or a shield?

But no one else dared to step up and fight,
Not the kingdom's guards or the even the knights.

So even though the Prince was scared he still knew,
That fighting the dragons was something he must do.

So he went to the King's bedroom and opened the door,
And went inside and walked across the floor.

He opened an old chest that was tall and wide,
Where the King had kept all his war gear inside.

The shield was big and the sword was so long,
It was no wonder the King had been so strong.

But the Prince was a boy, not a king like his dad,
And to lift up the gear took all the strength the boy had.

And that made the Prince get even more nervous,
And he wondered if he was ready for this service.

Fighting dragons was such a scary task,
The Prince, to himself, had some questions to ask:

How could a little boy ever be a man?
How could the little Prince ever make a stand?

But at the bottom of the chest there was a small note,
And it looked like something that the King wrote.

So, just when the Prince thought he was over and done,
He picked up the note and it said, "To my son."

He took a deep breath and opened the note he had found,
And this is what his father, the King, had written down:

To My Son,

If you are reading this now it means I am gone,
And you are the one that must carry on.
Our kingdom is now what you must save.
And to do that, you have to be brave.
I know that you think you don't know what to do.
But remember that I was once a little boy, too.
I was also small and had fear in my heart,
And I didn't even know where to start.
I couldn't imagine going over the hill,
To face the dragons that wanted to kill.
But don't worry son, you will be just fine,
If you can keep these things in your mind:
The dragons, they aren't really that big at all,
It is only in our minds that we make them so tall.
Inside our brains things always get overblown,
Especially things that are completely unknown.
But when fear settles in and gets a hold of you,
Here are some things that you simply must do:

Stand up straight and hold your head high.
And look at your fears right in the eye.
Don't look away and don't try and hide,
Know that you have great strength deep inside.
When you stand up and go into the fray,
You will feel your fears start to go away.
And though there will be horror you feel,
The things you are scared of are not a big deal.
This is not to say you won't feel a scare,
Fear is a feeling that all of us share.
Fear is normal for every person on earth,
But this is where a hero proves his worth.
A coward runs away when danger is near,
But a hero will face the thing that they fear.
So that is what you must do my son,
Face the dragons and do not run.
And I promise when you meet them you will see,
That you are just as strong as me.
The dragons that seem so mighty and mean,
Are not ever as bad as they might seem.
And most of things that fill you with dread,
Are usually just made up in your head.

- Your Father, The King

Now the boy was still scared, though not as bad,
After he got done reading the note from his dad.

The next day he got up and began to get ready,
He was still scared, but the note kept his mind steady.

Of course, he still felt some fear in his mind,
But he knew he would have to keep it confined.

And despite all the fear that he had,
He knew he needed to listen to his dad.

So he picked up the shield and picked up the sword,
And held up his chin, and he went out the door.

The people of the kingdom knew where he was going,
And the crowd in the streets, it just kept growing.

They stood and they cheered and they shouted and smiled,
And hoped the kingdom would be saved by this child.

And the Prince gave them a crisp salute,
As he marched past them all, down the main route.

And at the end, he stood up very straight,
And then he simply walked out of the gate.

Once outside of the kingdom, he tried to stay brave,
As he walked toward the Dragon Cave.

He could smell the fire of their breath,
And wondered if he would meet his death.

But he remembered what his father had said:
That most of the fear was inside his head.

When he got near the cave, he looked all around,
But he saw no dragons upon the ground.

So he walked closer and then heard some noise,
And though it scared him a bit, he still kept his poise.

Then he got to the edge of the cave and looked in,
And saw countless numbers of dragons within!

But when the dragons saw him, they scattered and hid,
Even though the Prince was just a little kid.

And the Prince, he couldn't believe his eyes,
Because to the Prince's great surprise,

The dragons, though many, were as small as could be,
In fact, they only came up to his knee!

And when they breathed fire, it was just a tiny flame,
That any little matchstick could put to shame.

And their teeth were very sharp and white and shiny,
But they were also so very tiny.

The teeth they had were as small as a pin,
And wouldn't even bite through the Prince's skin.

So the Prince walked right into the cave,
Just as a Prince and a King should behave.

And one small dragon came out looking sweet,
And sat on ground at the Prince's feet.

And the Prince was convinced by this little sight,
That his father, the great King, was absolutely right.

The fear was just like the King had said,
It had all been in the Prince's head.

So the Prince left the cave and headed back to town,
And all the people saw him come down.

They clapped their hands and shouted with joy,
That the kingdom had been saved by this boy.

The Prince climbed up and stood on the wall,
and this is what he told them all:

"There is really no reason for dread,
All of the fear is just in your head.

The dragons, they can do nothing to us,
And there really is no reason to fuss.

So have no fear of a dragon attack.
In fact, the dragons will never be back!"

And with that, all of the townspeople cheered,
Because the Prince had quelled the thing they most feared.

And the Prince tried to tell them the dragons were small,
But they wouldn't listen to him at all.

So the Prince carried on protecting the town,
And of course, he never let them down.

Because the dragons were so small,
They really were no threat at all.

And the kingdom carried on forever filled with laughter,
And all of the people lived happily ever after.

And that was the end of the Dragon Book.
And Mikey was so glad he had taken a look.

He realized something that he never knew:
If you are afraid, there are things you can do.

Instead of hiding or running away,
Stand up and face what makes you afraid.

And from that day forth, Mikey changed his mind,
And left his fears and his worries behind.

Even when he was afraid of something out there,
He knew how to get control of his fear.

He would stand up straight and hold his head high,
And like the Prince, look his fear in the eye.

And that is always the best thing to do,
If there is something that really scares you.

Don't get controlled by feelings of dread.
Remember most of the fear is just in your head.

This isn't to say you won't be afraid.
But you should know that fear is okay.

Everyone gets nervous and has a good scare,
And feels like they are going into the dragon's lair.

But when that happens and you don't want to go,
Think of the lesson the Prince got to know:

That when you are feeling so scared of it all,
You just need to remember that the dragons are small.

The End

ALSO BY JOCKO WILLINK AND JON BOZAK!

WAY of the WARRIOR KID

Available at bookstores everywhere. www.warriorkid.com

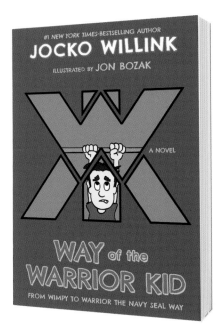 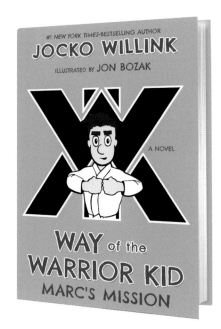

AND DON'T MISS...

WARRIOR KID PODCAST

Available through your favorite podcast player